Gritty at Fifty

Dr. Chitra Naik

Copyright © 2023 by Chitra Naik

All rights reserved.

This book or any portion thereof may not be reproduced or used in any manner whatsoever without the express written permission of the respective writer of the respective content except for the use of brief quotations in a book review.

The writer of the respective work holds sole responsibility for the originality of the content and The Write Order is not responsible in any way whatsoever.

Printed in India

ISBN: 978-93-6045-225-4

First Printing, 2023

The Write Order
A division of Nasadiya Technologies Private Ltd.
Koramangala, Bengaluru
Karnataka-560029

THE WRITE ORDER PUBLICATIONS.

www.thewriteorder.com

Edited by Ridham Bassi

Typeset by MAP Systems, Bengaluru

Book Cover designed by Keerthipriya PH

Publishing Consultant - Vaishnavi Nathan

Preface

Many events and incidents in our lives leave behind a lasting mark, stamping our hard disks forever. They leave us thinking, 'Why did I have to go through this?' Then you have a choice: To be compassionate and brood over it, or take the learning and build over them; To bask in the old laurels or keep building new ones; To stay fragile or be agile.

Inspired by real-life incidents from her clients, friends, and family members, Dr. Chitra started penning down short stories and her thoughts and takeaways based on her analogies.

As writing is quite a therapeutic experience, she kept working on her writing skills, and the love and immense affection she received from her contact sphere encouraged her to publish a book as it appeals to all evolving soul-searching readers.

Contents

Preface v

Foreword xi

1	Gratitude For People Who Weren't Right For Us	1
2	A Transformed YOU Can Transform A Few	3
3	We Don't Live In Our Houses	5
4	Why We Choose Whom We Choose	7
5	The Breakup	9
6	Trust The Timing	11
7	You Are What You Believe You Are!	13
8	Fullness In Emptiness	15
9	Little Cruelties – Large Casualties	17
10	You Haven't Come This Far Just To Come This Far	19
11	We Learn To Worry Less About Old Worries, When We Have New Worries To Worry About	21
12	Make A Choice To Take A Chance To Change Your Life	23
13	Bread, Butter, And Jam	25

14	Outdated Dates	27
15	Life Or Lifestyle!	29
16	How Do I Mind My Own Business	31
17	Convenience or Commitment	33
18	Cloves and Cardamoms	35
19	Mind Chatters - Mind Matters	37
20	Alter Your Outlook And Look Out	39
21	Turn The Page Or Close The Book	41
22	Sambar Rasam Payasam	43
23	Katti To Kitty	45
24	Light, Camera, Aaaaand Action!	47
25	The Only Certainty Is, There Are A Lot Of Uncertainties	49
26	Enjoy The Kriya, Nirvana Will Follow!	51
27	Log Kya Kahenge!	53
28	Every Scar Can Raise Your Bar	55
29	Beyond First Impression	57
30	Different Strokes For Different Folks	59
31	Dinner Date At Quarter To 8. Don't Be Late	61
32	Madam To Maid!	63

33	Dye Or Die	65
34	You Are Not Good Enough!	67
35	Pick Up And Pack Up	69
36	New Turn Or U-Turn	71
37	Why Fret Over An Empty Hat!	73
38	I'm Not, What I Think - You Think, I am!	75
39	Beggars Can Be Choosers!	77
40	Black And White, Or Gray	79
41	How She Wishes, The Wish, He Too Would Wish!	81
42	The More We Indulge, The More We Wish, We Didn't Indulge	83
43	Pants Or Pajamas	85
44	Tharoorification Or Simplification	87
45	Out Of The Box	89
46	Live Life Queen Size	91
47	Complement For Compliments	93
48	Inorganically Organic	95
49	Who Moved My Cake?	97
50	Classically Chaotic	99

Foreword

Who is Chitra? I bet that question danced through your mind when you picked up this book adorned with a captivating title. Let me assure you that Chitra, whom I affectionately call Chits, is as captivating as this clever title.

I am still wondering: is this the same girl who I knew from my school days, wearing a blue and black balloon dress and walking as if she is always jumping on her feet? My mind was always intrigued by her introverted yet very humbling demeanor, and to cut a long story short, here I am writing a foreword about her as my best friend, a friend that each one of us must have. Chitra means picture, and believe me, this picture is worth framing in your hearts and minds.

Sincere and humble at heart, Chitra, hailing from a simple conservative family, always aspired to make it big and used to be indifferent to societal norms. A rebellious sculptor of her own unconventional path, she is always aspiring to add more shades to her life's canvas. If you peel away the layers of her achievements, she is the same old school girl who still leaps about in my mind. I guess today I can decode this unique trait. She always wants more from her life, and her excitement to get more from every moment was her thrill.

I have observed her remarkable evolution spanning three and a half decades. Although she seems to be a bit timid on the exterior, I call her the powerhouse of resilience, grit, and smarts. Life for her is a bible of experiences and anecdotes, and that's why you will find her most of the time happily sitting alone, observing and meticulously sketching the curves and contours of her life. The idea to pen down her unique observations germinated right there in those confused and perplexed musings.

When she wrote this masterpiece, I could relate to each of her thoughts; they are genuine, they are transparent, and a splash of wit made them imperfectly perfect. As her nature is, she has kept this book very simple, with loads of sense and zero nonsense. A wise believer says, Don't teach anything you haven't learned yourself.

As unconventional as she is, so are her writing skills; it's like watching a movie where characters come alive sans make-up and any pre-written scripts. Every story in this book will surely remind you of a similar person or familiar situation, as this is just her real-life experience, which ends with hilarious, sometimes painful, yet truthful endings. Please do not expect every story to end like a Karan Johar-esque finale. Life unfiltered is much more attractive and real than the one we watch on screen. As a child, I always felt life should be more like movies, but today I feel movies should be more like life, and this book lives by this notion.

'Gritty At Fifty' is a 'Must-Read' book where you are the protagonist, juggling and wrestling with the vibrant chaos of your life and nailing it with your signature style. Remember, your fall always makes you tall.

Akshata Mahale
Leadership & Executive Development Coach

When I interacted with Dr. Chitra the first time, I found her in a bewildered state, amused about the answers to the questions she wasn't sure of. But as I began to know her better, I discovered her to be very diligent and honest in her work. Always exploring new things, she is extremely multitalented and fierce in her goals. She is as calm and composed as she is gritty and witty. Reading her blogs and articles is an absolute treat to the mind and soul, with interesting takeaways.

An absolute 'Must Read' book, 'Gritty at Fifty'.

R.S
Advocate

1

Gratitude For People Who Weren't Right For Us

Karan Bindra, founder of one of the leading fashion brands in the city with more than 100 outlets all over the country, had an appointment at my skin clinic. He had scheduled this appointment for his anti-ageing treatments with me two months in advance. I prepared the procedure room and ensured that he receives the best hospitality. I was waiting for my fellow colleague, Dr. Rita, to join me for the procedure, as I was performing it for the first time. However, I couldn't reach out to her on the phone, which left me feeling anxious.

When I returned to my consultation room, I found a voice message on my phone from Dr. Rita saying, "Dr. Rita here; I can't make it today due to an unexpected emergency. I'm sorry for any inconvenience. I hope you understand." It was evident that she was excusing herself every time, as it was her fourth last-minute cancellation without any backup substitution.

I was reluctant to accept such unprofessional behavior and felt helpless, given the challenging situation. But after a while, I took a deep breath and proceeded with the procedure. Not only did I perform it diligently, but I also received excellent feedback from Karan.

I let go of the anger I had directed at Dr. Rita due to my initial frustration because the two-hour ordeal had tested my abilities and ultimately made me more confident and capable.

Often, the behavior of certain individuals is nearly intolerable and unacceptable to us. We feel that they have disturbed our lives completely. However, we fail to realize that such people bring out our hidden potential, helping us grow and adding new dimensions to our lives. Whether they betray us or harm us, they play a role in changing our destiny. They make us strong enough to independently deal with the challenges and become exemplars. In disguise, they are like angels, guiding our growth and leading to positive changes in our destiny.

From that point on, I began to practice gratitude, even towards people who initially seemed wrong to me.

2

A Transformed YOU Can Transform A Few

When I was young, my mother had a lot of self-created problems. She wouldn't sleep, and she would often feel exhausted. She used to be irritable and grumpy. Then, one day, we noticed a change in her. The situation remained the same, but she had transformed.

My brother, who had a tendency to procrastinate and waste time, was preparing for his IIT JEE exams. He said to her, "Amma, I may not be able to crack three subjects."

Amma replied, "Okay, no issues, son. You may do well, and if you don't, you can retake the exams. In the meantime, also find a source of income to pay for your studies."

My sister, who had started working at an MNC just a month ago, said, "Amma, I'm quitting my job. I can't work for nine hours a day."

Amma responded, "Okay, work for twelve hours at home, although you won't receive a hefty paycheck for it."

We were puzzled by her responses. Amma used to typically nag and push us to do things. We suspected that she had seen a doctor who might have prescribed her a dose of 'I don't give a damn 1000mg.' She might have taken an overdose.

When we asked her if she was on some anti-anxiety medication, my Amma explained:

"It took me a long time to realize that each person is responsible for their own lives. It took me years to discover that my anguish, depression, insomnia, and stress did not solve their problems but only worsened mine. Therefore, I concluded that my duty to myself is to remain calm and let each person solve what corresponds to them. So, from now on, I cease to be the receptacle of your guilt, the advocate of your faults, the wall for your complaints, or the one who should solve your problems or shoulder your responsibilities."

My brother not only cleared his JEE exams with flying colors but also pursued his M.Tech., and my sister excelled in her career.

One can only intervene in one's own life. You can't change anyone else. If you could, you would have already done that. The only person you can change is yourself. A transformed person can transform a few..

3

We Don't Live In Our Houses

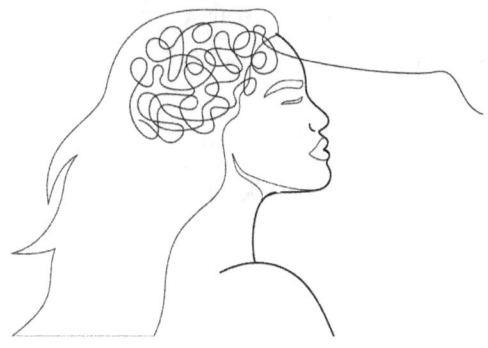

I once asked Dr. Murtuza, "How do you maintain your focus and sharpness during your 4-5-hour-long surgeries, especially in your late 50s? Don't you get too drained?"

Dr. Murtuza, one of the top surgeons in the country in his field, performs on average 2-3 surgeries per day. He is also an avid reader, an eloquent speaker, a connoisseur of music and the arts, and a singer—truly an inspiration to many.

His humble reply was, "My surgical instruments don't know my age. You need to prevent yourself from stopping yourself. Every game in life, whether played in the operating theater, your procedure room, or on the playground, is actually played in our minds."

He continued, "If I had kept my mind full of hatred growing on the operating table, regrets and resentments accumulating in the corner, expectations climbing to the ceiling, and worries scattered all over, I would have been forced to retire a long time ago. The key factor to performing exceptionally in every arena of life is the ability to control the quality and quantity of your internal dialogues."

We don't live in bungalows, duplexes, or 2BHK or 1BHK flats. We live in our minds, which is an unlimited area. You can explore and live your life to your eternal potential when things are sorted and uncluttered in your mind.

4

Why We Choose Whom We Choose

It was a cold evening. Ella had a busy week and just wanted to take some time off for herself. She headed to 'Jazz by the Bay,' the elite pub in the city. Ella looked gorgeous in her black shirt, dress, and pumps. while in the pub, Ella came across Stavros. Stavros was one of those guys who exuded sexuality and could send a woman into overdrive. Ella, a strong-willed and successful single woman, was taken by surprise by the rush of attraction she felt for a stranger. They exchanged numbers and after a few conversations, started dating each other.

She found herself getting swept away by a bad boy again. Ella had craved love as a child from her emotionally unavailable parents, so she believed this behavior was normal.

Dating Stavros for a month added a lot of drama to her otherwise lonely life. Ella enjoyed the roller coaster of emotions and the thrill involved in dating Stavros, who always came up with surprises and lived on the edge. She couldn't resist the excitement.

However, Ella soon realized her life was becoming chaotic. She discovered that Stavros was manipulating her and hurting her with his arrogance and self-righteous behavior making Ella lose her identity. As her conscience woke up, she finally broke up with him.

The new Ella, with a calm and poised demeanor and oozing confidence, began to attract good men who treated her with respect, the way she deserved to be treated. Ella was now content in her own company after decluttering her life from toxic relationships and deodorizing her thoughts.

`Ever wondered why we choose whom we choose? People and experiences in our lives are reflections of our thoughts.

5

The Breakup

Lately, we could no longer connect with each other the way we used to. In the past, we would talk endlessly, laugh, and cry together over the silliest things. Every emotion and inner thought was understood, acknowledged, and empathetically addressed without words.

But now, our friendship had lost its charm. Even occasional connections had become more of a duty than a heartfelt bond. Sarcasm had replaced the delightful banter, and bitterness and resentment were the predominant ingredients. Then, one day, during a so-called petty disagreement, we had a heated argument, and we said our goodbyes. Ego had clouded our judgment. Either of us could have made an attempt to call and reconcile, preserving our 25-year-long friendship. However, we didn't because, the question "Why Me?" had taken over. To say I was blindsided and heartbroken is an epic understatement.

When we talk about heartbreak, it's often in the context of romantic breakups, where the infamous spark fades away. But what about that one best friend who knows every vulnerable part of you and is meant to stand by your side? What you share with your friends is different from what you share with your partner. It's raw, authentic, and 100 percent you. They are the ones you can confide in about your achievements and setbacks, and you can repeatedly complain to them, even if you're annoying them. They're supposed to be your cheerleading squad, your safety net, and your agony aunt. You find solace in sharing a few words with them each time.

You go over everything, especially the deep secrets you shared with them, and suddenly there's an epiphany. You remember the look on their face and the quiver in their voice, and you wonder how you never noticed it before or how you never wanted to consciously accept it!

How in the world could I have been so blind?

Situations change, people change, and our tastes change. Sometimes it's better to gracefully accept change, take the lessons learned, and exhibit self-sufficient competence. Move forward with gratitude for their valuable contribution to your life at some point, which has shaped you into who you are today.

The new you is unbreakable after a breakup.

6

Trust The Timing

Kaira had a wonderful, high-paying job. But then came a time when the company was downsizing, and she was slain. Her eyes were unfathomable with oblivious emotions. She asked herself, 'Why me?' Her personal life was also going through turbulent waters. Her stars weren't in her favor. She couldn't find a suitable job for quite some time. The experience was quite devastating for her. Meanwhile, she started learning various dance forms, something she always wanted to do. Her dance classes kept her upbeat and in high spirits despite her otherwise low life conditions. She excelled in her performance and started assisting her dance guru in the classes. Soon, she personally started tutoring many students and gradually opened her own institute. She started enjoying her newfound passion, and before she could even realize it, she had become a successful choreographer. She never had to look back at her mundane corporate work again.

Ever wondered why things happen only at a specific time?

Everything in life happens for a reason. Only later, when a wonderful thing happens, does one realize that, if the tragedy hadn't happened in the first place, this wouldn't have fructified. Failure and tragedy are a part of nature's chisel, chipping away at us in an attempt to improve our lives. But only if you can turn the mess into a message for yourself!

Kaira was trying to survive the emotions that had engulfed her. But later, as she started discovering her passion, she realized that this precarious situation was meant for her to thrive again, to create her own identity, and to be venerated. It's funny how things can really alter your trajectory if you embrace them and do not run away from them.

Many times, we wonder, 'If only I had done that differently, then it would have been different' No... whatever happened is the only thing that could have happened. Nothing could have been any other way, and it happened for us to learn, evolve, and propel. Every situation that we encounter is perfect, even when it defies our understanding and our ego. Everything begins at the right moment, neither earlier nor later, because we are subconsciously ready for the new experience or challenge only after the old event.

7

You Are What You Believe You Are!

Rachel met Joe in her office, who came across as a vibrant, exuberant person. As a person fresh out of a relationship, she wanted to forget her heartbreak. Rachel liked his outgoing personality and his sense of humor. She used to feel flattered, and her broken heart seemed to be healing with Joe's affection. She just wanted someone to assure her that she was amazing because her self-esteem had come down after her past experience. They start dating.

Being with someone else doesn't necessarily mean you are 'over' someone. It could be a way of compensating; it could be in vengeance towards your ex.

Soon, she started noticing that he was too manipulative, but Rachel wanted to give her best, and she thought, with her love, she might change him over a period of time. The very first time she wanted to go out clubbing with her friends, she was made to feel guilty for spending time away from him and also for coming home late in the night when he himself would stay out all night without any valid explanation.

Joe would hang around with his girlfriends very often. Once, when she caught him red-handed, he gave a quasi-apologetic apology without actually feeling apologetic and instead got her into a guilt trip, making her responsible for his drift. Very often, he would twist the previous conversations to defend himself and rather make her feel as if it's her fault to be forgetful and ridiculous.

Joe had a way of walking into the room and dragging a dark cloud because he wanted attention and focus on him, and he made sure every person in the room noticed that he was angry, discontent, and unhappy because he was a big-time attention seeker. Rachel would scramble herself to make him feel comfortable. He would often try to intimidate her with outright abusive language, anger, and temper tantrums to control her and get his way out.

Rachel felt delirious, emotionally drained, and lost her self-confidence after being in a relationship with Joe for 5 years.

She realized that she was compromising her beliefs to accommodate him. She realized she was being manipulated and overpowered badly, and her willingness to give herself completely for the relationship was rather taken as her weakness and exploited.

She rewrites her life and takes charge of her own narration with her new beliefs.

You are what you believe you are!

8

Fullness In Emptiness

It has been more than seven decades of freedom. But does political freedom or economic freedom give us freedom from our thoughts? Because it's our thoughts that can make or break us. Very often, uber-successful CEOs and celebrities are more prone to depression than their average counterparts. At times, extreme success has so many strings attached that it can completely pull a person down and somaticize them. There is extreme competition and unnerving feelings of failure. Many times, the human touch is lost as we are climbing the ladder. There are no more face-to-face conversations. We hide and seek escape behind small screens, a Bluetooth device, or earplugs—seeming to always be connected to somewhere far away from the here and now. Despite new modes of communication, we are psychologically becoming islands isolated from one another.

Actually, there is something very comforting about being a regular Jack and being one of the pack. Extreme success and the time and effort that it takes to get there can make life seem precipitous and lonely. There is something very soothing about sailing in the same boat, bitching about similar situations, government, taxes, and bosses, and the way we were all empathizing with each other during the lockdown. But the moment it's pulled up, the elitist and brightest of all take a big jump forward, and the whole scenario changes. The simple things, like family dinners where the discussions are about family, like Raghu hitting me and Meenu taking my notes, that bring pleasure and joy to life, are lost because we are consumed in constant work or business and growth 24/7. Extreme wealth and fame, when they come suddenly, can make us feel detached from our own identity. Many times, even when people achieve their goals well on time, something they had always dreamt of, by the time they reach there, although their finances look great on a sheet of paper, their values change by then, which hardly seems any gratifying and leaves them empty and hollow.

Sadly, in today's world, money, success, and fame rule our lives at the cost of our health, relationships, and peace of mind. Materialism and consumerism are driving us. There is nothing wrong with seeking money and fame, but if this defines our relationship with money, we could be on the slippery slope because somewhere we are losing sight of what is more important in life than money. There is rather more severe bereavement in losing loved ones, losing friends, losing health, losing spiritual connection, and losing purpose in life.

So, can we seek freedom from our negative thoughts? Because when things change inside you, things change outside you. You seek fullness even in emptiness.

9

Little Cruelties – Large Casualties

Serena and Williams sat on the couch with the lawyer applying for divorce. They had many good reasons to stay together: their cute son, a plush house, and a history stretching back to the good old days. But why was Serena insisting on divorce?

Williams planned his boys' trip when she was longing for a family outing, which was conveniently forgotten.

It sounds so frivolous and stupid on one level, but perfect on the other. Serena felt her opinions and views weren't valued. Her preferences and choices were ignored. He would escalate every ordinary disagreement to a major crisis, giving her silent treatment for days. He had the habit of blaming Serena every time anything went amiss, right from a balky laptop to a rained-out picnic. He would snap at her whenever he had a bad day, and then she would distance herself from him further.

Are these casual cruelties, careless words, and thoughtless actions worth ignoring? After all, it's the small things—casual passings, accumulated weights of small hurts, flashes of anger, small betrayals—eroding love and goodwill.

Emotions can be disastrous, but if they are attended to, connected, and expressed well, we can make the best use of our internal compass and the camaraderie between relations, which can be beautified with a little sensitivity, thoughtfulness, and caring. Otherwise, little cruelties can cause large casualties.

10

You Haven't Come This Far Just To Come This Far

For the past six months, Meera Mohan has been on the verge of leaving her stressful corporate job.

She is tired of trying to maintain a positive attitude during workplace idiosyncrasies and enjoying a silent chuckle when confronted with the unexpected, bizarre, incongruous, and ironic things that happen all the time. While working on the PowerPoint presentations and spreadsheets every single day, she would grapple with questions like, 'Why is the job so unfulfilling? Am I crazy, naïve, ungrateful, immature, and stupid to think of quitting this lucrative, paying job? But as she keeps analyzing the situation, she realizes that the path leading to this corporate job was like following the herd, but if 'I leave the job, as mad as it sounds, it would be the truly active decision ever taken.' And one fine day, she decides to walk away from things that no longer align with her thoughts and quits her job to pursue her dream of opening a boutique with no plan or strategies in mind.

Women, especially in India, have long struggled and have been made to believe that they can't achieve anything on their own. This makes them dependent on their father or husband, and as time moves forward, they even suffer identity loss. They lose their confidence to make better decisions for themselves, feel frustrated, and are often lost.

Meera Mohan gets into the dilemma of either stepping back from her dream for her not-supportive family or standing up for her vision. She finally decides to listen to her own voice and her own soul instead of listening to the noise of the world.

Without any support, raising the business on her own becomes an unending nightmare. But because she takes this plunge against her family's wishes, she starts leading a masked life as a successful entrepreneur. She really feels hurt when her ex-colleagues and friends are having extravagant weekends that she can't afford to enjoy her weekends like they do. Finally, she comes to terms with her predicament, decides to let go of what everyone thinks about her, and regains the courage to stand alone. She becomes minimalistic externally as well as in her internal universe. When one is in need of money, it is easy to cut corners, compromise on values, and deliver a subpar product or service. But her continued pursuit of growth while retaining integrity and the constant seeking of improvement keep her going, and her boutique starts flourishing gradually.

Now, when she looks back on her struggling years, she feels that if the journey wasn't challenging, the destination wouldn't have been so rewarding.

Achieving a goal is a wildly exhilarating thing. If you are fighting with the idea of giving up, you could be throwing away something wonderful—your best future. After all, **you haven't come this far just to come this far!**

11

We Learn To Worry Less About Old Worries, When We Have New Worries To Worry About

Many times, we are preoccupied with thoughts like, "Did I do right?" "Could I have done better?"

They are such familiar thoughts that they are in our system without our awareness. To even stop worrying, we first need to be aware of how often we carry the burden of our past behaviors, even when we think we are done doing them. "I don't know if I replied to his or her message effectively", "Did I make a fool of myself by confessing my mistakes and my truths?" Often, these situations niggle our thoughts, and we start losing our sleep over them until some new worries take over the old ones.

Here's a short story that beautifully explains this:

Two priests were returning to the temple in the evening. They came across a young, beautiful girl (seemingly new to the city) who was unable to cross the busy city streets. The elder priest walked up to her, held her hand, and got her across the street.

In the evening, the younger priest asked the older one, "Sir, as priests, we aren't supposed to touch a woman."

The elder one replied, "Yes, brother."

The younger one, totally puzzled, asked, "How did you get her to cross the street?"

The older priest smiled and said, "I left her on the other side of the road, but you are still carrying her!"

In the course of life, our mind is constantly flooded with thoughts. It's constantly judging, evaluating, and trying to make sense of life's events. What about the relationship we share with our thoughts? Can we change it to help us deal better? Gentle detachment from the thoughts and focusing on the present can help you accept and let go of what you cannot control and move forward.

Instead of living in terror of an external adversary, it is time to strengthen your immunity, harness your psychological stability, and use your intelligence to become part of the solution, not the problem.

After all, overthinking and replacing new worries with old ones is not time-worthy!

12

Make A Choice To Take A Chance To Change Your Life

Caroline walked into a pastry shop with her mother and was bedazzled with the array of treats on offer.

'What should I choose? What should I choose? What should I choose?' Caroline said to herself.

"Come on, Carrie (Caroline's pet name), we don't have a whole day to spend on this," said her mom.

"I want this! No wait, I want this!"

Caroline walked along the aisle, unable to make a single choice.

"Quick, Carrie," said her impatient mom. "We got to go."

Frantically, Caroline's eyes moved around the shelves, but all the options looked so good that she couldn't choose one.

Eventually, her mom picked up young Caroline and walked out of the store empty-handed. Caroline had her tears running down profusely as she wanted all of them but couldn't choose one.

Life is like a pastry shop, displaying a myriad of choices at every phase: career, relationships, and investments, but, in the fear of making the wrong decisions or in the absence of timely advice, if we can't decide for ourselves, we will end up empty-handed.

13

Bread, Butter, And Jam

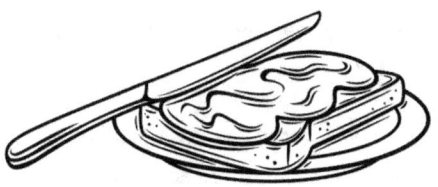

Just about when life started seeming normal, the second wave of the pandemic struck more badly, and once again, we were all locked up indoors unwillingly.

Every morning, waking up to the rising number of COVID cases, getting more paranoid about it, binge-reading books, and binge-watching Netflix other than office work and housework became a regular routine. Nothing seemed exciting; unlike the first lockdown, Dalgona coffee and banana cakes all seemed to have lost their charm.

After months of staying cooped inside, the blissful 'work from home' seemed increasingly intolerable.

After my second jab, I straight away wanted to hit the roads and be with friends. So started the friends' coordination and late-night thrilling discussions for a short getaway.

Finally, we, a group of 10 friends, came together, of which 2 backed out.

Here comes the most interesting part of the trip planning. While I was researching the best service apartments, one of the superhosts offered free bread, butter, and jam along with tea and coffee. The freebie offered by the superhost, however meager and trivial it sounds, had a priceless effect on me, and I immediately zeroed in on that property because it reflected the thoughtfulness of the host. And needless to say, the property, the stay, and the host—everything just happened to be fantastic.

After returning, I introspected: If receiving a freebie is so exhilarating, can giving it away freely be even more ecstatic?

We all wish to be liked, accepted, and loved. But we cannot receive what we do not give. If we sow generously, we will reap generously.

A random act of kindness, being a mentor to someone, or being just there for someone can be some of the delightful freebies we can practice freely daily! What can be your freebie delight? Free bread, butter, and jam today!

14

Outdated Dates

Why do we tend to hang on to so many things till they are done and dusted?

I was making my favorite Caesar salad. I reached out to the frozen canned olives from the fridge and topped them with virgin olive oil, amongst a few other ingredients. I started eating too noisily, champ-chomp, as I was too starved. While the salad seemed delicious, the olives tasted weird, spoiling the entire taste of the salad. I checked the olive can, and to my utter surprise, I discovered that the can displayed an outdated date.

The incident got me thinking about how we hang on to so many things in life that have actually ceased their shelf life. We stack unwanted ropes, clothes, bills, and medicines endlessly in the unstated hope that, in some unspecified future, they may serve some unguessed purpose. Our instilled behavior of not discarding things that no longer have any utility goes beyond tangible objects.

We tend to dwell on overdone and dusted events, which rots our thoughts and impacts our future dealings. Many people come into our lives with an expiration date to either give lessons or experiences. The earlier we accept it, we can create a window for richer experiences and stop staled olives from spoiling the salads further.

Beware of outdated dates!

15

Life Or Lifestyle!

Nanda: Tu aj kya kar rahi hai ? Seedhey nikalke Vashi aja. Let's have lunch and go shopping.

Nandita: Aati hun. But post lunch, because you know na, I no longer have a battalion of servants and drivers. I will have to wind up the housework and come. So I will try to reach you by 3 p.m. You do shopping while I do window shopping; I need to do my monthly budgeting. But I will enjoy it!

Nanda: Oh ya I forgot, that's really sad. You must be going through a tough time.

Nandita: Not at all. I am perfectly fine. Earlier I had a lifestyle. Now I have a life!

Young, ambitious Nandita had a high-pressure corporate job. To earn that fat paycheck, she used to start her day early, travel for at least 4 hours a day, and be left drained with no time or energy left for herself or her creative side. She had blazed job satisfaction. In her pursuit of achieving competitive goals, she missed out on the little daily joys of life. So she quit her job and started her own business.

Today, after 5 years of quitting the job, does she regret the decision? No. Why? In the challenging process of starting from scratch and building her own setup, she learned so much about the business and discovered herself. She gets enough time to explore new things that were a farfetched dream earlier, which makes her feel so much more alive. After all, pursuing your own dream is so much more gratifying than pursuing your boss's dreams. After all, it was her choice to choose peace over paisa.

Today there is fast food but slow digestion, good luxury cars but lack of good roads, steep profits but shallow relations, social status but declining self-respect. Speed, materialism, and competition have become the social markers of progress, which come at a price.

As our lifestyle improved, life's challenges were replaced with lifestyle challenges. At times, we have to choose between life and lifestyle if one is sabotaging the other.

16

How Do I Mind My Own Business

Nanda and Nandita gossip every evening. On one such evening, Nanda hastened up to the terrace in her crumpled kurta and unlaced walking shoes, with her earphones struggling to stay in her hands, as a feeling of dread followed her. As usual, she hurriedly called up Nandita..

Nanda: kya yaar! Mere bal pakk rahe hai. Budhapa aa raha hai.

Nandita: Tuney Pooja Bhatt, Tabu ko latest webseries mei dekha hai? Wo ab kaunse jawan dikhte hain. Phir tu kis khet ki muli hai? Shanti rakh.

Nanda felt relieved.

The next evening ...

Nanda: My husband thinks he is such a perfectionist! I am fed up.

Nandita: You know na, mere pados wale handsome single uncle? Once I met him during my walks. While talking to him, I finally asked him, "Uncle, how is it that you remained single? Did you never like anyone?"

He said, "Me, being a perfectionist, I wanted a perfect wife." I counter-asked, "So, in this whole world, you never found any?"

He giggled and said, "After my retirement, I found one perfect woman. But she was hunting for a perfect man!"

Nanda got the message and felt relieved.

The voyeuristic nature within us wants to observe others, their habits, their styles, and their thoughts and ideas. What is it about similarity? What is it about fault-finding that engages us? Ah! The comfort of gossip—a few words shared in confidence with a byline, 'don't tell anyone'—makes us feel like the closest, most confidential, and righteous person on earth.

Gossiping is so comforting; it gives reassurances, releases worries, intensifies bonding, helps networking, and at times it can even be educational.

In this competitive world, how do I mind my own business when your business is much more interesting?

17

Convenience or Commitment

Ring ding ding da ring, the alarm bell rang. It was 5:15 a.m. But I was already up, waiting for the alarm bell to ring right at 4:45 a.m. I had an even busier day today. But I didn't want to compromise on the morning routine. So, I did a brief exercise act to kill the guilt of not exercising and immediately cooked my favorite breakfast.

I had been contemplating commitment or convenience for the past two days. My heart wanted to stay in the comforts of the home, catch up with my regular clinic routine of attending to a few patients, and read and listen to music. But I had committed to my club friends to participate in a tree plantation project. The sultry weather outside was highly discouraging. But I thought that if I choose convenience over commitment, the burden of guilt would leave me remorseful. Time was up, and my friends started calling me incessantly. I indecisively made peace with the situation and met them at the meeting point.

As we reached the village, the villagers welcomed us with their traditional greetings. The club members had done some incredible selfless work there over the years, and the industrious labor-intensive villagers had diligently worked hard towards the tree plantation project. A great deal of pertinent information worth more than ten years was being wedged into such a small window of time between the club members and the villagers. But I could barely be part of the zeal and enthusiasm of the people around me, as my whole focus was on the ascending mercury and the unbearable scorching heat.

As we started driving back home, I realized that commitment can only be felt when it exceeds convenience. If everybody had to choose convenience like me, the whole new transformed village wouldn't have happened. Our attitude towards convenience and commitment determines if we are mere consumers or contributors.

Convenience can lead to incompetence, while commitment gives a sense of fulfillment.

18

Cloves and Cardamoms

As she was searching for a new series to get hooked on after her clinic hours, Nandita's curious eyes got stuck on Chesapeake Shores. The sight of an undulating landscape, rolling hills, lush greenery, and the sophisticated family, around which the story revolves, transferred Nandita to another world altogether, where she aspires to be. But, as she watched merely two episodes, the series seemed a little boring as there was absolutely nothing thrilling. Everything seemed perfectly inconceivable, and she started losing interest.

Nandita was lately struggling to feel happiness. She was getting consumed with the thoughts of an uncertain future. She was feeling depleted of energy, and she lay on the bed flat, like her phulkas. Determined to straighten up her life, she strode herself to the local kirana store. She bought a variety of spices and basmati rice to cook her favorite soybean pulao. She used to love cooking her meals. She was full of passion and creativity. She pondered: When did she stop loving herself? Meanwhile, her neighbor dropped in. They had a hearty chat over the chai session.

During the course of time, her heavy heart lightened up. What would life be without uncertainties and ups and downs, which are actually like cloves and cardamoms in her pulao?

Joyfully sipping her evening adrak cutting chai again, and sitting by the window, Nandita thinks she has gotten used to her hurting back and knees; she has gotten used to her bifocals, but if she gets used to being stupidly mindless and stops enjoying the ebb and flow of life, she will miss out on the spice of life, and it would become pleasantly inconceivable, like the first episode of Chesapeake Shores!

19

Mind Chatters - Mind Matters

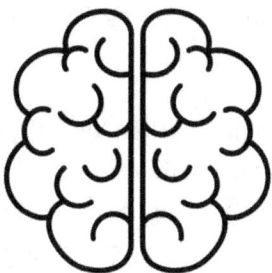

When you are in an empty house, loneliness is palpable. It gets even louder when you hear your neighbors frolicking and celebrating the festivities with their families. Even while everyone revels in the sights and sounds of festivities, for the homesick, it's the most deafeningly quiet time of the year.

The sun was not bright. The clouds were covering it up, making it a calm and gentle afternoon. It was a festive time. To distract herself, Nandita stepped out for window shopping. On her way to the city mall, the psithurism of the trees in the breeze could hardly calm her clouded mind today. Some kids were throwing stones into the puddle of water, enjoying the sight of the muddy water splashing dirt everywhere—something that Nandita used to play joyfully as a kid. But today, the grimace on Nandita's face was unshaken. In the mall, she started checking the clothes as if she was doing some audit with no intention of buying. Her groggy tone and low demeanor irritated the store manager. She then entered a bookshop and bought some books. She thought she would dwell in the books until others were dancing to the tunes of the festivities.

After reaching home, she brewed her filter coffee, and while sipping it, she immersed herself into the content and characters of the book, inviting herself to the literary world and distracting herself from her anxious mind. After a while, her clouded mind became calm and gentle. The sky was too bright.

When the water in the puddle is muddy with unnecessary sediment, it's inappropriate for usage. Similarly, when the mind is muddy with unnecessary sentiments, it's inappropriate for usage. Reacting to a disturbed mind is like throwing stones into muddy water, which splashes out only dirt. Give it some time to grieve and settle down when the clouds uncover the mind and bring it back to its brightness. As time passes, the chattering mind declutters its dirt, and it minds only what matters.

20

Alter Your Outlook And Look Out

Nanda is conducting a half-hour free webinar training with one of her clients today from 2 p.m. to 2:30 p.m.

At 2 p.m., Nanda is struggling with her low wifi connection. She tells her attendees, "Sorry for the technical glitches", a message she herself is tired of saying every time. At 2:10 p.m., everyone is struggling with audio issues. At 2:15, Nanda manages to get a grip on her Zoom platform. The fact that she is never able to fix these technical issues and start her virtual training on time has been her source of chagrin every time. By then, all the attendees lose interest and put their videos off. As the webinar is over, Nanda walks around the room, stomping her feet and putting aside her laptop, seething with rage. She wants to give up her maddening training job.

Nanda then remembers her pre-decided Zoom tea meeting with her besties, Nandita and Usha. A time stickler, Nanda logins at sharp 3 p.m. Typically impatient, Nanda gets restless with the other two logging in late. She starts fidgeting with her laptop mouse. After a while, when Nandita logs in, Nanda growls at her.

Nanda: Nandita, why on earth are you late for a Zoom meet too? Were you busy putting on your patent red lipstick?

Nandita: For a change, I was combing my hair, and the hair fall is making me so tense.

Nanda, with her thick volume of hair too, complains, "I too will get bald soon."

They both engage in a vain attempt at consoling each other's frustrations.

Meanwhile, Usha logs in with a scarf tied to her head. Usha is going through some severe medical treatment in which she loses her hair completely. But she seems to be largely unaffected. Smiling and giggling all the time, Usha seems to be as lively as ever. She expresses her gratitude that she is alive and is hopeful that she will regain her hair.

These days, Nanda has been getting overwhelmed with every little thing. Her self-created unhappiness was manifesting dissatisfaction everywhere else. Usha's resilience, despite her catastrophizing experience in life, is an eye-opener for Nanda. She changes her outlook and looks out for happiness within and in her surroundings.

21

Turn The Page Or Close The Book

Arun's wife, Sheela, asked him, "Aren't we going to Pop Tate's today despite it being Friday?" Arun hardly raised his head from the laptop and said, in his hoarse voice, "No. I have lots of work." The next day, Arun was busy organizing a blood donation camp at his club. Sheela was missing the weekend fun. She was missing the mall trips, the food court junking, and partying with her friends. Arun used to be a gregarious person. But over the months, Arun's personality was changing, and Sheela was stuck to the old story she was holding about Arun.

Their relationship started unraveling over petty issues. After a few months, they barely acknowledged each other as they hardly shared any common interests. They loved each other, but Arun was in search of a more meaningful life. Partying seemed frivolous to him. Sheela was in search of an answer to make the changing paradigms of her relationship with Arun work.

One day, Sheela noticed a Kalnirnay calendar hung behind her kitchen door. It was still showcasing January in the month of September. In a jiffy, Sheela felt like closing the open calendar and discarding it, as it had been of no use, and over the nine months, the entire calendar seemed to be clogged with dust and looked hazed brown. But as Sheela turned the page to the ongoing September month, it looked unvaryingly fresh, untouched, and bright. Sheela had an epiphany. She unwillingly started taking an interest in Arun's charity work. Gradually, she started liking it, as it gave her some sense of gratification. One Friday, Arun lovingly gave a special treat to Sheela at Pop Tate's.

Two individuals together create a third entity, a relationship. As the moods, emotions, experiences, thoughts, and feelings are in a constant flux, there are times of disintegration and discontentment, followed by times of appreciation, warmth, and contentment. We all have unacceptable, unlovable, and unreasonable parts within us, but if we uncover the clogged and dusted upper shell, chances are we may discover the brighter, acceptable, lovable, reasonable, and untouched parts of the person, like the Kalnirnay epiphany.

At times, turning the page can be more self-discovering than getting stuck on the old page or closing the book.

22

Sambar Rasam Payasam

"Thodi chai pilana," said Arun to Sheela. She had just come from work after a very hectic and tiring day. Quite irritably, Sheela hung her dupatta on the kitchen door knob and started making tea noisily. After sipping the tea, Arun lay on the bed and started watching an IPL match. Sheela got busy cooking in the kitchen. Her kurta was drenched in sweat. She was standing next to the hot pan, making dosas. She called out, "Arun, khana laga diya." Arun jumped on the bed, and said, "Sixer! Sixer!" After a few seconds, he came out of his chilled AC room.

While having his meal, he remarked, "The sambar is too spicy." After dinner, Arun dozed off to sleep, while Sheela was still busy winding up the housework. She started thinking, 'When will this work get over?' She went off to sleep without worrying about the unending homely chores or about the next day's meals and tiffins.

Why is she the first one to wake up in the morning and the last one to sleep in the night? The house is not just her responsibility!

After two days, Sheela left for Goa for the annual conference for seven days. Arun felt the house was quite untidy. He was tired of swigging all his meals. He missed Sheela's masala tea, which was his evening bliss after a tiring day. He missed her sambars and rasams.

Once Sheela was back, Arun started helping her with household chores. He took her out for lunch at Ramanayak because Sheela loved their payasam.

After fifteen days, Arun, disgruntled in his AC room, said, "Aiyo, all out!" At the dinner table, he muttered, "Rasam is too bland! He then went off to bed while Sheela got busy with household chores and the next day's meeting presentation work.

'Men will always be men,' sighed Sheela, exasperatingly.

71 percent of women in India sleep less than their husbands, according to a survey. Caught in work-life balance, trying to be the best everywhere, they end up doing work-life integration.

Should men always be men?

Can payasam be as often eaten as sambar and rasam?

23

Katti To Kitty

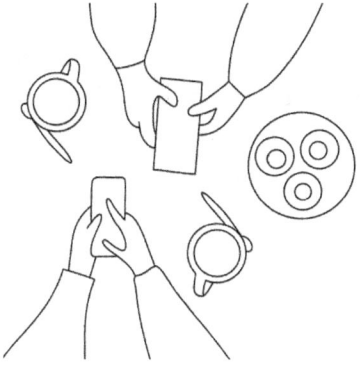

Nandita is getting too bored at home today. She has been contemplating attending a kitty party hosted by her friend, Neha, for some time. Today, she thinks, let me checkout for once. Nandita wears her favorite gray-colored sari, which is the navratra color of the day. Normally an unflustered sort of person and mostly never unsure about anything, Nandita heads toward the restaurant. It's a Saturday afternoon; all the tables are full, but she notices the noisiest table. Neha and a group of 6-7 ladies are chattering and laughing away in high spirits in unison.

The ladies are flaunting their Esbedas and Baggits and Bibas and Libas. The prattle of voices becomes louder and faster, and Nandita finds it difficult to keep up with the pace. This is one of such situations, where she feels so tongue-tied that she has nothing to contribute to the conversations. Thankfully, after 2 hours, there comes the bill, and the ladies start prodding into their branded handbags. Some pull out their credit cards; others pull out their cash. The sound of rustling notes is a welcome break, and Nandita lets out a sigh of relief.

Nandita feels no connection with this environment or with the kitty party ladies. Everything seems too frivolous and fake. People are blowing their own horns; she decides not to join the form.

At times, being in a crowd can make you feel lonely when you don't belong to the crowd, even remotely. And being alone can bring you solace without any population.

She makes her mind, Katti to Kitty.

24

Light, Camera, Aaaaand Action!

As I walked around, examining the set and outfits, I smiled to myself. Everything seemed perfect, exactly the way I had imagined it. I walked up from the dressing room to the front stage. I was hosting a chat show to be aired on a national TV channel. The show expert was rehearsing her lines. The tech crew was busy fixing lights, cameras, mikes, and props. My makeup was a bit overdone to contour my aging face. But that didn't bother me, as I was living one of my dreams. As I gathered my composure, a voice came, "Camera Rolling!" The clapperboard showcased, 'Zindagi Ek Safar, Scene 1 Take 1'.

Director, Sidd, said, "Aaaaand Action!" Within 20 seconds, he intervened, "Cut! Cut! Cut!" My presentation was fairly good, but Sidd's attention was on my irritating, frizzy strand of hair popping out. Being new to this profession, my focus was on improving my fumbling lines, while Sidd's focus was on the hair, the sari crease, and general wear. We finally arrived at the desired outcome after a few retakes.

Life imitates art. In real life too, no two people experiencing identical events will interpret those events in the same way. We will each place our own nuance, importance, relevance, and ultimately showcase the event the way we perceive it, resulting in different images being projected onto our two different screens.

Unforeseen and unfavorable events will keep rolling. Adjust your lights and cameras from irritating frizz to illuminating glitz and action your retakes until you arrive at the desired outcomes.

Action can turn illusion into vision!

25

The Only Certainty Is, There Are A Lot Of Uncertainties

It was a chat show with a psychiatrist. We were chatting about schizophrenia, a mental disorder characterized by scary hallucinations, paranoia, and disorganized thinking. During the course of the chat show, one of my questions was: After treating the schizophrenic patients, are there any relapses? He answered wittily, "Yes! The only certainty is that there are a lot of uncertainties."

Why, in life, are we so resistant to uncertainties? Isn't settling for a comfort zone forever and refraining from challenges like settling for cowardice? Aren't we resisting life if we are resisting change?

Look at it this way: when we watch 10 episodes of CID, everything becomes so predictable in the 11th episode that it loses its charm. You enjoy an ostensible suspense thriller only when the situations are menacing and you are at the cliffhanger till the end.

Why not treat life in a similar way? Harnessing the power of uncertainty can allow us to find courage instead of stunting our growth by staying in our comfort zone.

I was ending my chat show by saying, "Dekha, darshakon, kaise aap doctor ke ilaaz se ek behtareen zindagi jee sakte hain!" The doctor laughed his heart out and corrected me. "Your doctor can only give you tablets, counseling, and shock treatments. It is up to you to turn your scary hallucinations into earthly actualizations, absorb shocks smoothly, thrive back healthily despite uncertainties, and make your zindagi behtareen."

It is so rightly said, 'Why match-fix your life when you can rather enjoy the game?'

26

Enjoy The Kriya, Nirvana Will Follow!

I was sitting on my favorite couch corner, gazing at the sky hopelessly. With her gym bag in one hand and protein shake in another, Khushi said, "Aw! Mummy, why don't you go on a solo trip or just gang up with some like-minded buddies and just explore? You will feel better." I gave some thought to Khushi's advice and realized that it wasn't a bad idea. After all, what's wrong with sparing some time for oneself and relaxing? I felt elated at the very idea of going on a trip. When she was back from the gym, I told her happily, "Yay! You are my best buddy, Khushi. Why not explore together? We will paint the town red!"

Our Google search started from Dalhousie to Mount Abu to Kutch to Mahabaleshwar and finally settled at Goa. We had a whale of a time until late at night, researching the best economic places to stay and the nearby activities, until our search, which started from Ozran

Heights to Beach Resort to Ciroc Hotel, finally settled down to Nirvana Hill Resort.

When we imagine the most blissful part of our vacation, we picture ourselves with a drink on a beach, tapping our feet at a bar, or stumbling across an enchanting waterfall on a long drive. But the happiness and excitement begin way before, during the process of planning and visualizing yourself there, the detailed study of the place, and the innumerable negotiations with all the travel associates.

Enjoy the process and the journey, as having something to look forward to heightens your energies. You can work happily even after a tiring day because the building up of positive expectations and excitement actually gives a different kind of high and soothes our mind over any discrepancies, even if, in some unforeseen situations, results don't quite measure up to our fantasy.

We started visualizing the ultimate nirvana at the Nirvana Couch, sipping our drinks, gazing at the sky, and planning our next Dalhousie trip!

27

Log Kya Kahenge!

I would call my dressing style a mix of sassy, pixie, and classy. Many times, people don't get my personality. But I like to stay unpredictable. They think I dress up to attract other people. But no, that's not true; I dress up as per my moods. When I feel happy, I dress up accordingly to show my confidence. When I wish to shy away from people, I dress up like 'behenji'.

While people cast their judgments on almost everything, women majorly bear the brunt, as they feel the pressure to balance a sexy feminine appearance with a conservative girl next door approachability and often even wear a corporate look.

One day, I just decided that I won't get distracted with 'log kya kahenge!' It was a sultry, sunny day. I wore a white cotton salwar kameez to beat the heat. I paired it up with flat sandals. I booked an Ola to reach the clinic. A maid servant in the lift asked me, "Madam, aj aap kaam pe nahi ja rahi hai?" I replied sarcastically and sheepishly, "Nahi, main kirana ki dukan mein ja rahi hun." As I sat in the Ola, I was getting irritated and distracted by her remarks. But soon, I reminded myself of my decision and tried to carry myself like a confident intellectual, the way any doctor would do. But in reality, I was feeling too powerless.

The next day, I wore a blue dress and paired it with heels; I was feeling confident. An old colleague of mine bumped into me after three long years. She exclaimed, "Hey gal! You are looking as slim, sassy, and classy as ever." At once, it elevated my mood. I said to myself, 'Log kya khub Kehte hain!' Her opinion answered the questions my inner self was fighting off: 'Have I gained weight? Are my curves still in place?'

We are constantly exposed to a steady flow of opinions, unsolicited advice, and judgments. When we love being appreciated, should we disregard being occasionally degraded?

Should we get distracted or should we adapt to "Log kya kahenge"?

28

Every Scar Can Raise Your Bar

Wearing my red Nike shoes and comfortable track pants, my feet strode out to the joyful rhythm of Carpenter's songs. As I was greeting and putting up some fake smiles on a few familiar faces, my nostrils frowned suddenly as a ghanta-gadi passed by. As I walked ahead, it left its fetid, stinking smell far behind. I was in two minds about taking a U-turn and going back home, but I quickly sneaked out to the first by-lane for some fresh air and completed my 5-kilometer walk.

In the office, when Eric asked me to find another job, as they were downsizing the company, I was having self-deprecating thoughts. My brain started fabricating a story to calm down my emotionally threatened mind.

'All I have is me, and I can only count on myself,' I said to myself, because in such situations, you are scared of your nearest ones being preachy and judgmental, however good their intentions are. I quickly sneaked out into a by-lane, which opened out a plethora of self-discovering opportunities.

And now, as I have completed five progressive years, I have realized that if I had stayed there longer, the fetid, stinking smell of office politics could have created more emotional scars.

A career downfall can be a getaway to a new highway.

Every scar can raise your bar.

29

Beyond First Impression

Infinite blue sky with fluffy white clouds, warm breeze swirling around me, sending my hair in all directions, humidity giving me a sauna effect, waves lapping on the shores creating a foamy effect around the gray sand, firangs moving around in sarongs, children building sand castles, light music touching my ears from the beach shacks—I was going to revisit these memories even after a decade during my forthcoming Goa trip.

As I sat on the balcony of a hill forest resort in Goa, sipping my blissful morning tea, I could not get my eyes off an alive forest astir with life, rays of mellow sunlight filtering through the canopy, penetrating through the leaves, the fresh aroma of leaves and drizzled rains and wet earth, birds twittering... was completely different and beyond my first impression of Goa.

During my initial interactions with the resort owner, I found him flirtatious, so I restricted my interactions to formal dealings, discouraging any off-track conversations. When I met him at the resort, I kept my guards high, being apprehensive of his intentions, and restricted my conduct to polite pleasantries. But, as we engaged in periodic small talks, I discovered him as a genuine, helpful person during the course of my short stay there.

Research shows that, within seconds of our first interaction with the person, our brain starts developing the first impression of the person, and at every subsequent encounter with that person, our brain focuses on confirming that first impression. But actually, we can discover so many hidden layers of the person, which can be so much different or better than the first impression.

If Goa can be beyond beaches, isn't every human personality a culmination of different pieces? The question is, isn't it at our discretion to expand our horizons and explore beyond the first impression?

30

Different Strokes For Different Folks

Being month-end, I was broke, but Nanda insisted on going to the Designer Expo at the World Trade Center as she wanted to buy some wedding jewelry. As I was checking out different stalls, by the time I stepped out, I had picked up three saris, thanks to an unobtrusive but extremely effective salesgirl who not only understood my taste but also had just the right amount of persuasiveness in her interactions. Given their different customer profiles, persuading a mere browser to become a buyer and understanding their psyches so that they don't come across as garrulous and annoying interferers but as helpers is an art.

On the other hand, Nanda didn't buy anything as the salesman at another counter was busy arranging and least interested in selling. Also, maybe because she was wearing a dowdy outfit that day, the salesman thought she was incompetent to buy his stuff!

While we are parenting, we are constantly trying to sell the values that we believe in to our children. Children are constantly trying to sell us their wants and needs. We never box our children into being dowdy or rowdy. But while dealing with outsiders, our minds get cloudy, and we forget that human personalities aren't just one-dimensional.

As we are all salesmen throughout our lives—selling our ideas, concepts, values, services, and products—do you think we need to use our masterstrokes for every bespoke? We need different strokes for different folks so that every casual browser becomes a loyal buyer!

31

Dinner Date At Quarter To 8. Don't Be Late.

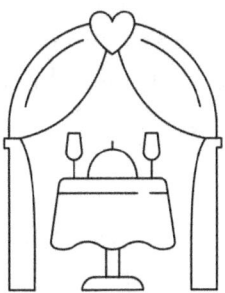

Karan parks his Mercedes at Starbucks. He calls out for his favorite cappuccino and starts working on his laptop as he reaches 7:15 p.m., half an hour early. As he is busy drafting an urgent proposal, his phone beeps—a notification from Ritika: Sorry, I'm stuck in traffic. It looks like it will be half an hour.

As the coffee is placed on his table, Karan dives deep into his thoughts. The heat of the coffee radiates into his fingertips. He stares at the intricate leaf design floating at the top of his cappuccino. Karan pictures Shona sitting across his table with a goofy grin plastered on her face while moving her manicured red nail-painted fingers in her beautiful, lustrous hair.

Married to Shona for 13 long years, their marriage had hit a plateau. They used to be irritable and criticize each other's disturbing habits.

Shona used to hate Karan walking around the house in his office shoes, and Karan would get irritated at the unattended laundry lying on the bed the whole day. With household and financial responsibilities, the interest to try anything new had disappeared. Karan was looking for some adventurous spark outside of his mundane married life. So, he had struck up this first date through the Tinder dating site. But as he was waiting for one long hour, he felt guilty for going stray from his 13 long years of married life.

The temptation to look for love from a third person when the attraction between the partners hangs by a thread can be hard to resist, but the damage can be irreversible.

As Karan sits back in his car at 8 p.m., he writes to Shona, 'Tomorrow, dinner date at quarter to 8. Don't be late.'

32

Madam To Maid!

I walked up the clinic in my stylish pencil formal black skirt, paired with a gray shirt and black shoes. As I entered, the front desk staff stood up to greet me. The nurse walked after me to my cabin with a patient's file and asked me, "Ma'am, shall I call the patient to the procedure room?"

In the evening, as I reached the studio, the makeup artist walked after me, made me sit on the hot seat, and asked me, "Ma'am, shall I give you a quick touchup on your face?" The shot went very well. The director said, "Pack off!" One of the crew members asked me, "Ma'am, shall we call for Ola to drop you off?" As I sat in the car, I couldn't stop smiling at myself for the various successful hats I was wearing.

As I reached home in the night, my daughter walked after me to the kitchen and nagged, "Mom, when will the dinner be ready?"

No matter how many hats we wear outside, the moment we step inside the home, we are first: mother, sister, wife, and daughter. And nobody can take that place. So leave all the hats at the showcase. As working women around the clock, we never truly clock out the day; we simply remove one hat and replace it with another—from Madam to Mom to Maid!

33

Dye Or Die

Nandita is engrossed in her book. She has been reading for an hour now, sitting on her favorite couch in her ruffled nightdress. It is 8:30 p.m., and she has called it off for the day. Meanwhile, she receives a call: "Hey! How are you? Long time! I am in your town, around your area. Mind joining us for dinner?" Nandita hides her face with her hands while talking to him. She walks up to the mirror. She looks at herself through her dark brown eyes; her glow has faded with the passing time. Her eyebrows are unkempt. She runs her rough hand through her frizzy, no-dyed hair, further disheveling it. She is in a dilemma; she would rather die than show herself in an unpresentable look. Feeling disgusted about her appearance, she tells him, "Oh! I am so sorry! I will be late from work. Can we plan this next time, maybe?"

Nandita had just read a post on LinkedIn that said, 'If you would rather interview a candidate over food, so many traits and aspects of the candidate could be learned, which may not be evident while in the office.' She imagines how she will be judged first based on her appearance before being judged on her handling of a fork, spoon, and knife.

Every time a girl is told she looks cute or pretty, she is actually being told that she is being looked at based on her appearance. Whereas boys are more likely to be assessed on their personalities like being outgoing, adventurous, smart, shrewd, etc.

When will we become badass? When will we embrace ourselves the way we are? Will we ever live fully in the moment or die dyeing?

34

You Are Not Good Enough!

Always well-updated on stock markets and meticulous in her dealings, Nanda visits her financial advisor's office for ITR filing. While going through her papers, he remarks, "Your financial planning isn't good enough. Inflation hasn't been factored in. You need to reallocate your funds." Otherwise a self-assured, Nanda gets baffled to learn this.

On her way, she visits her cosmetologist friend's clinic to rant about the financial advisor's comments. Her friend gives her a patient hearing and remarks, "Your skin isn't good enough. Your skin is sagging as you age. You need to take a few laser sessions."

As she steps out, she remembers that her dentist had told her a month ago, "Your teeth aren't good enough. Go for teeth veneering."

A pretty confident and self-righteous Nanda suddenly feels the imposter syndrome.

She tries to figure out whether she is imperfect. She ruminates, 'To gain traction, marketers try to attract the so-called, unattractive, imperfect customers, expecting them to get attracted to their unattractive schemes!' Should she allocate her funds to the marketing gimmicks of an unending list: cosmetologist, dentist, finance specialist... and experience diminishing marginal returns, or be tough enough to not fall prey to the worldly specialists trying to show you that you are not good enough!

35

Pick Up And Pack Up

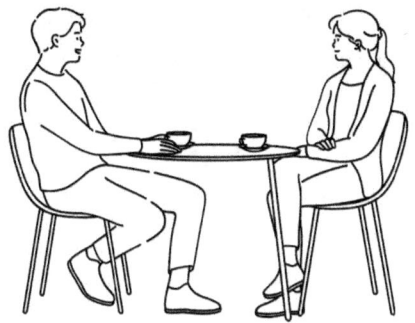

It was a Friday evening. Karan drove Nandita down to the nearby café. His staid, sober personality was always very calming. His dark-rimmed glasses made him seem more sophisticated. As he was having his cappuccino and she was sipping her green coffee, he generally updated her about the day. She was hearing him without listening to him. Her mind was preoccupied with all the future uncertainties. Trying her best to hide her tears and put up a strong front, she was constantly blinking her eyes, looking here and there, trying to hide her pent-up emotions; she was spinning her finger ring, "ahem," clearing her throat. They finally left the table with unspoken words, feeling the deafening silence between them despite the pounding, gurgling espresso machine noise and the vibrant hustle in the café.

Whether it is a relationship, friendship, or something beyond those realms, it's generally understood to talk about things before picking up the pieces, packing up, and moving on. But at times, you no longer feel the necessity to lash out the anger and frustration because, for a long time, unfulfilled promises and unfulfilled expectations leave you with no words and no hopes.

She looked for assurance; she looked for actions that would eliminate the emptiness within. But, contemplating her dream for stability to trade with endless hope, she walked away, leaving words once again at the tip of her tongue that remained unsaid.

36

New Turn Or U-Turn

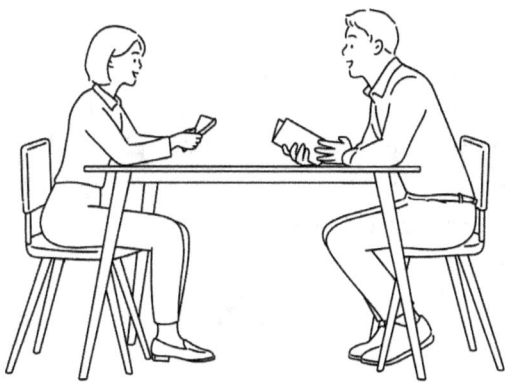

Nandita finally winds up her last appointment at the clinic and rushes to the café. She is already late for her scheduled meeting with the producer. As she enters the café, her eyes get stuck on someone sitting at the corner table; she had met that person five years ago. She gets into the meeting with her film producer friend.

As she takes her first sip of green tea, her mind gets transported to the time five years back: He walks in his blue jeans and black Nike t-shirt, with the car keys clinging to his jeans. She is waiting for him at the corner table. He fakes a warm smile at her. As she is trying to express herself, he is squeezing his eyebrows together. He has a nightly Kolkata flight to catch. He is scheduled to see someone there and move on with her. But Nandita is finally falling for him. This time, she badly wants to give the relationship a chance. He had made his best attempt to convince her of the relationship while she was taking her own sweet time. Meanwhile, things had gone downhill. Either the consequences of their unknown actions or their fate struck a dismal picture of their future, compelling him to move on. But now the tables have turned. How she wants to stop him! But there is no more room for follies or mistaken findings. He looks around the room speechless and leaves indecisively.

While she had turned left and he had turned right, while she felt the pain of a new turn in her life, she contemplated the sweet pain of hanging on to the hope of his possible U-turn. But later, she realized that this new turn was a blessing in disguise.

37

Why Fret Over An Empty Hat!

"Yes! The artwork will be sent by the end of the day," says the ad agency guy. It's already been 2 days, and Jessica is still waiting, juggling the magazine printing deadline with the production department, her boss, the editorial department, etc. Huge amounts of money are involved, and Jessica's job is at stake. The endless, expectant wait gets too late, and finally the magazine gets printed, leaving Jessica in a miserable state.

"Yes! I, too, want to travel around the world. Her boyfriend marks a tick on her wish list, written on the paper napkin, while they are dining at a restaurant. It's already been 2 years, and Jessica is still waiting to see any plans or even intentions to travel. Huge hopes are involved. Her world is divided within the four walls of the house.

Quite often, despite knowing there seems to be no growth in the current job or despite knowing the relationship isn't heading anywhere, we continue to hang on to the feeble thread of hope, thinking we would rather take what we can get than deal with the horror of being jobless or single. It's a band-aid for an open wound that doesn't heal because it can't. All talk and no action serves one purpose: to make sure the statuesque stays right where it is. All that talk buys is a lot of time in anticipation for something better to come along because what is there now will never be sufficient. Talk becomes the 'hope', and passive inaction becomes the 'reward'.

"A cowboy with a big hat but no cows isn't really a cowboy at all."

Then why fret over an empty hat?

38

I'm Not, What I Think –
You Think, I am!

On the dance floor, sweaty, drunken teens are jumping to the base of the music. At the bar, a group of friends slam a shot glass down. Dressed predominantly in black, people are gathered in cliques. Jessica, in her carbon black cami, paired with a dark wash skinny denim skirt and pointed toe heels, enters the bar. The place is too noisy and dimly lit, with mind-numbing, eye-watering smoke suffocating the breath. Jessica stands against the wall, feeling completely out of place, waiting for her friend to arrive. As she tries to groove to the music, her eyes suddenly get stuck at a table; four men are glaring at her. Jessica feels her heart pounding; she feels like running home and burying her head in pillows. Some deep-seated suspicion starts clouding her mind: What must they be thinking I'm?

Everyone likes to think they are a good judge of others' character based on their clothing style and lifestyle. We tend to see others' choices and behaviors as indicative of their personalities or characters in all situations rather than the result of a temporary external situation; however, we fail to reflect on our own lives.

While at home, Jessica was feeling a puddle of anxiety from uncertainties mixed with a thundercloud of loneliness. To beat this feeling, she had planned to go clubbing with her friend. But even in the pub, Jessica muses unhappily, 'How is it possible to be in a crowd and still feel so alone?' As her chin quivers and tears threaten to spill over, she reflects, 'You can't blame situations and people until you can triumph over your own thoughts and fears, as they will chase you everywhere, even if you change jobs, places, or partners.'

With this sudden epiphany, Jessica glares back at the four men, and her inner voice says, 'I'm not what I think—you think I'm!' And she goes back home, turns off the light, and crawls into her bed in contention.

39

Beggars Can Be Choosers!

Being in and out of relationships seemed like intermittent fasting to Kiara. Her soulmate search looked like a salad bar—a little bit of this ingredient, a little bit of that topping, dressing on one side with all the idiosyncratic ingredients in one.

What is it that makes us discontent with our forever-wandering thoughts, frustrations, innumerable fears, unfulfilled desires, unaccomplished tasks, and futuristic dreams? We try to find all the answers in one ideal partner, who doesn't exist. So, can beggars be choosers?

As he walked in, Kiara noticed this devil-may-care, outstanding personality. He was a dapper with a deep voice and an extensive depth of knowledge on a multitude of subjects. Kiara was certainly impressed with his capability of striking a lucid conversation. But he seemed to be a too-freestanding, self-contained person.

'Will there ever be a strong, deep connection given our way-different backgrounds?' questioned her wandering mind.

Just because the plate is empty, should someone settle for a Caesar salad with basic lettuce leaves and garlicky croutons, or should it be topped with a creamy dressing made with eggs, olive oil, and other idiosyncratic ingredients for a fulfilling experience?

Her wandering mind answered that beggars can be choosers!

40

Black And White, Or Gray

"Two large Black and Whites with 2 ice cubes, water, and soda," said Reagan as the waiter leaned forward to take the order. The rustic ambiance of the open terrace bar, with rich and distinct music playing behind it, set a perfect conversation mood between Reagan and Clara.

On a nearby table, there seemed to be a business deal. Amidst a seemingly serious discussion, the man lit two cigarettes and offered one to his lady counterpart.

Clara's eyes glowed as they lay upon the woman, puffing. Reagan questioned, in disagreement with Clara, "What about the man burning off his lungs too? What about you sitting here and having alcohol? What is right for you can be wrong for her too."

Being right puts us in a scrutinizing mode. We look for evidence to prove other people are wrong rather than considering their opposing views. Our brain is under constant pressure to either justify our thoughts or hide our flaws. Being right is a paradox. Reality is a byproduct of our perception. We all watch the same movie, yet each one of us remembers different things as per our beliefs and experiences in life. Being right is a fluid concept that needs to evolve with time.

Life is never black and white. With the addition of soda and ice cubes, we can experience the depth and richness behind the range of ambiguity within the different shades of gray.

41

How She Wishes, The Wish, He Too Would Wish!

Karan is impulsive, quirky, and fun. At first, Kiara inspired him to embrace life in the moment whenever he felt dejected by the unprecedented challenges thrown at him. Not that her life has been easy, but it's a conscious choice that one can make every day to feel content and hopeful by emphasizing the brighter side rather than feeling dejected by the darker side of circumstances.

Failures can make one more resilient. Although one may never get over the big heartbreaks in life, with days and years, one can become more empathetic toward others because they can relate to them through their own experiences. Authenticity and transparency are so hard to come by these days when people mask themselves with a superficial side of theirs! Despite new ways of communication, psychologically, we tend to become isolated islands until we find our true soulmates.

Many a time, she would wonder, 'How I wish I had met this amazing guy before; life would have been so different and so much more beautiful.' But whatever happened was the only thing that could have happened. Nothing could have been any other way, and it happens for one to learn, evolve, and propel. Every situation that one encounters is perfect, even when it defies our understanding and our ego. Everything begins at the right moment, neither earlier nor later, because we are subconsciously ready for new experiences only after the old events.

Her burning wish to meet this intelligent walking encyclopedia increased when, once, his dark-rimmed glasses, which made him look more aware and powerful, made her feel stilted, where she appeared frozen with a cushion on her lap, not willing to leave him ever!

Her bigger wish is to love each other's unlovable parts and to accept and compliment each other's imperfections perfectly, making them a perfect team.

How she wishes, the wish, he too would wish!

42

The More We Indulge, The More We Wish, We Didn't Indulge

With Gucci/Fendi, perfectly blow-dried hair, immaculately manicured nails, and designer labels top to bottom, the socialites were sipping tea amongst the spread of sandwiches, cakes, etc. at the high tea party. There were mothers choosing suitors for their daughters; rivals trading veiled insults in polite singsong tones; and influencers carefully choosing whom to be seen around with, as per the perceived social strata of the designer label owners. One thing was common: women were posing their best to click tons of pictures to flaunt on their Instagram.

While some were born in the lap of luxury, others had earned their share of success in their respective careers through their flair for networking, perseverance, and knack for attracting attention, adulation, and applause from every quarter. It was interesting to see them navigate their world of affluence, superficial friendships, and emotional ups and downs; their spats, ego tussles, and power play within the circuit of the actual reality show. Some of them were discussing the venue and makeup artists needed for the next party.

What was missing were deep, soulful conversations. Clearly, some people were feeling intimidated by others' power plays.

The longer we are caught in the cycle of consumption, the more natural it seems, and the wheel keeps spinning with no finish line without any realization that these stressors are so self-inflicted. The more we indulge, the more we wish we didn't indulge!

Can real human connections be displayed, downplayed, or labeled? Can Gucci and Fendi feel more trendy with a positive human vibration frequency?

43

Pants Or Pajamas

While window shopping, Zara is always on my hit list. The display is so irresistible that you want to try out those pants, although you hate seeing the exorbitant price tags. The pants that fit your tiny waist will pull hard into your crotch, trying to accommodate the big booty. If you try bigger pants, they will just slide off, giving the look of pajamas. Which means you have to walk into the fitting room with every kind of pants. I can't discount the discomfort of the attached pins, clips, and tags, like Basanti dancing on the glass. Then the stress test of sitting down, ensuring that the stitches of the pants can outlast the pressure of my extraordinary figure and posture. 'Will they shrink? Will I fit into them after dinner? What kind of optical illusion will make me look slimmer? Will I get good comments on social media? Am I trying too hard to look young, being forever in denial of my aging age? What should I weigh more, charisma or comfort?' After all the trials and discomforts, I move on to Marks and Spencer, not knowing a similar disappointing experience is awaiting.

On Jeevansathi.com, can a hotty display honesty? Can a stunner display good character? The freedom to keep on exploring options, basking for a while in the initial beauty of attraction, and discounting the forthcoming discomfort of attached hot and cold life's spins and whips can make you lose your grip on the right decision-making. Can charisma shrink over time? But love can outlast the pressures of life! After all the trials and discomforts of stress tests, should you move on to Shaadi.com, where similar experiences could be waiting for you?

Should the endless search for an 'Extraordinary' go on or make yourself extraordinary?

Comfort or charisma? Pants or pajamas?

44

Tharoorification Or Simplification

Joshua, an aspiring pilot, has his radio telephony exams scheduled. One of the evenings, as he is gazing at the books while trying to attempt this unintelligible subject for the third time, he displays crabbed irritability, serving self-cynicism. His disillusioned state of mind pulls him to attempt playing football, hoping to alleviate his exasperating mood. While playing, an unobservant Joshua develops racking pain in his right shoulder. Although the pain is unbearable, he tries to bear it by gulping self-prescribed painkillers for a few days. Resting all day long in severe pain, he becomes a glutton, gaining several pounds, which compels him to postpone his scheduled class 1 medical test further.

Why, that is, can a person conquer the corporate ladder, become a militant CEO, demanding the respect and admiration of hundreds of brilliant minds, and then flounder through a simple dinner date with a beautiful stranger? Do we complicate simple things in life by overthinking and losing our vision in the process, like in the case of Joshua, who went into a negative spiral of thinking leading to a disillusioned vision and got distracted from his ultimate goal? Our outlook toward our goals can be unhelpfully constrained by our past experiences, which can mean we chase our tails by merely being active instead of being effectively productive and creative.

Don't use a big word when a singularly unloquacious and diminutive linguistic expression can satisfactorily accomplish the contemporary necessity.

Wait, did I just get inebriated with the exuberance of verbosity?

Why 'tharoorify' a simple sentence? Why complicate simple lives?

45

Out Of The Box

Sitting at my table, I was a complete deadpan after a long working day, wondering, 'Should I call off the day?' There enters a high-spirited marketing guy. He starts giving me unsolicited gyan. 'Ma'am, so high is your credibility, but so low is your brand's visibility! It needs some instant mobility.' He was trying his best to create a need when I was displaying disinterested greed. Since I was out of my mind, I wanted the nagging marketer out of my sight. I sighed out of relief, "Think out of the box and come back," when I actually never wanted to see him again.

After a month, he came up with a big brand strategy. I suddenly felt elevated, as if I were CEO, HUL, or P&G of the like.

He: Ma'am, we will integrate these SEOs;...00 will be your CTR.

Me: Where is the CTA? Haven't you thought of content marketing? Please get into the box before thinking 'out of the box'.

When people want to do nothing, they keep shutting down your brilliant ideas, dodging you.

To tackle this smarty, I would brush up on the marketing jargon, study the market well, and study my brand category well. I started putting skin into the game. Patiently listening to my unsolicited gyan, during his 4th visit, he was in my procedure room, undergoing treatment for his alopecia, and he further got me three more of his clients.

Actually, the dispirited and unmotivated me wanted an evangelist, not a market analyst. When I was shunning down his ideas and dodging him, I was actually dodging the dispirited me and shunning down my own growth. He got me into the box to think out of the box, and I got rid of the box.

46

Live Life Queen Size

Every weekend, I'm in a dilemma of which hat to wear today: 'Money saved is money earned!', or 'You live only once; live life Queen Size'.

As I was about to enter the cafe, my phone beeped a notification, 'Getting late. Just started. Water logging. I may reach there in an hour.' These put me in another dilemma: sitting and consuming 10,000 calories alone, waiting in the cafe, or going shopping, walking 10,000 steps!

I hated every store salesguy telling the same scripted sales dialogue: 'Yeh tumpe bahot acha dikh raha hai!' making me feel like a pretty lassie while other shoppers are busy scanning and judging you. Nevertheless, I ended up burning my pocket with a Rs. 100,000 bill.

Meanwhile, my phone beeped: I'm in the café. Where are you?' Finally, we came together to sit and judge others together. As we went chatty over the coffee, I realized that, before the coffee, I hated people. After the coffee, I love people, the check, and the transport. I paid off the check and went home feeling the Monday blues, wondering, 'Do I go to work so that I can afford the clothes, the shoes, the bags, and the accessories required to continue going to work?'

As I woke up on Monday morning, blue was the sky, and so was my mind, with clear goals and dreams to pursue. I picked up my phone just to check the time and ended up wasting so much more time checking Whatsapp, Instagram, Facebook, and also my bank account—far lagging behind for a weekend—queen size life! Meanwhile, my phone beeped a notification from my financial advisor: 'Be a smart investor. Stay invested to curb the inflation..' But I don't understand; if I'm selling, someone is buying. How are we both smart at the same time? A fine is a tax for crossing the line. A tax is a fine for doing so. But what if I'm paying tax without paying a fine? Which hat do I wear? Recession! Inflation! Depression! When my stocks are forever in liquidation! I think I should go shopping to curb this depression!

47

Complement For Compliments

By 8 a.m., when I'm about to step out, I hurry up to my neatly arranged yet overtly stacked wardrobe, where my sneering disdainful silk stoles on the top are struggling to balance their feet on the top out of arrogance, feeling insecure about maintaining their unearned top position, and my humble grounded linens, feeling incompetent at the bottom, are quietly trying to climb the ladder. Not to forget, at one corner, there are boxes of neckpieces screaming for attention: 'I complete you!' I spend a good 15 minutes glancing and mentally pairing up my tops and bottoms, putting everything together as per my mood for the day and the occasion, and choosing comfortable footwear to sync with all these. I realize that 45% of my clothes haven't been worn in two years, 25% aren't appropriate for any occasion, and 5% are what I actually wear on a regular basis.

I have a typical day meeting similar clients, presenting similar ideas but quietly expecting different results, and trying to climb the success ladder while competing with each other. In the evening, I meet a few like-minded, grounded gray chicks loaded with gray cells from different backgrounds presenting different creative ideas to raise funds for a noble social cause where each one complements the other for a collaborative common goal, where the neckpieces and the linens don't compete with each other but are in sync and complement each other. The communion happens to be quite an exhilarating and inspiring experience.

Are you spending 45% of the day worrying about the destination? 25% of the day is spent worrying about your limitations, 25% of the day is spent worrying about the competitions, and you end up doing 5% of the work again and expecting different results! Each one can complement and collaborate for a secured position and win compliments! Where the left foot steps forward, don't feel disdainful about the right foot, and the right foot behind doesn't feel incompetent, as it is catching up and both are balancing the top-earned position together.

48

Inorganically Organic

The sound of my growling hunger pangs was louder than the ultrasound in the procedure room. Later in the night at home, as I was settling down for the most anticipated peaceful time of my day—dinner time—I switched on one side lamp, placed my bowl of curd and cutlery, switched on my favorite program on Netflix, created the perfect mood... and as I was about to stretch my legs and switch on the AC, the remote control started acting funny, refusing to start the AC, until I banged it twice—thrice to the sofa. Then, as I was about to put my phone on silent mode, there came a notification: 'Tomorrow, are you attending BNI training?' I'm so used to putting up inorganic plastic smiles during the high octane meetings and trainings, that I instantly replied, 😀 . Then, finally, as I was about to have a bite of my savory, paneer-capsicum-masala, and rotis, I noticed that my delectable food had just gone through a baptism to brick-masala, as my client had just educated me, 'The branded inorganic chili powders are made of powdered and processed bricks. I imagined gluten cementing the bricks together to organically construct the inorganic wall alongside the inner lining of my innocent intestine, making me nutritionally deficient. Suddenly, my uncompromising meal time seemed so compromised!

Then, while hitting the bed, my restless mind felt the urge to emotionally connect to someone. So, I got into a chat with my bestie:

Me: The day was so hectic and tiring and...

My friend: ☺

Me: Mind talking?

My friend: ☹

She answered and ended my 30-word chat with two tiny emojis. In an always-online world, leaving someone on 'read' is a cardinal sin. In such times, emojis come as saviors when they help us avoid 'seen-zoning' and also reduce the burden of replying in words. When your friend sends a long message and you don't have the emotional bandwidth to respond to it, but you feel the pressure to respond, you acknowledge it with an emoji.

While staying stuck behind the perceived safety of screens—laptops, mobiles, instant messaging getting redundant to emojis—are we organically constructing inorganic walls within relationships? Are gluten-free, emotion-free, and inorganically becoming organic? Making the uncompromisable ecosystem so compromised!

49

Who Moved My Cake?

The feeling of every ounce of the sensory liquid spreading through every millimeter of her tongue was sending shockwaves, diving deep into every millimeter of her body. The sweet, bitter aroma of the beans was making her crazy with an intoxicating frenzy feeling, as she was allowing the richly dark contents of the creamy, frothy cold coffee with an extra scoop of ice cream to explode herself after torturous 14 days of having warm lemon water with honey in the morning, where all that she lost was 14 lemons and a bottle of honey and 14 days. So she started unfollowing her diet plan, as the diet plan was unfollowing her weight loss plan.

Khushi lazily ensconced herself into the lazy bag in her study room with dim light at 10 p.m. after an early dinner that she had at 7 p.m. The dinner was an orange broth with carrots, beans, corn, and cabbage. As she resumed her aviation phonetic studies, 'Alpha Bravo Charlie Tango Tree Fife Niner...' her disturbed mind suddenly got distracted when her eyes spotted an Instagram post of a new café serving crunchy waffles, pastries, and cakes, creating turbulence within the airspace of her stomach, growling and craving desserts. She convinces herself, calling it a last cheat day, as she indulges herself in the dulcified dessert. With a sudden spike in dopamine, she came back to 'Alpha Bravo Charlie' happily.

When the propeller un-follows the pilot's configurations, no matter the ATC's instructions to take off the runway, the aircraft can't take off a millimeter. When the mind un-follows your instructions, no matter the fad diet plan, the instant gratification urge will defeat the sustained long-term motivation where you can't take off the weight-loss, inch-loss journey.

'From tomorrow, I will exercise, I will do my walks, and I will go on a strict diet. I will go on salads. Oh! Wait, Honey, is there a Swiggy offer on cakes, donuts, and waffles but not on salads?'

50

Classically Chaotic

I entered an exquisite room, welcomed by an enthusiastic host. The classical music in the background created a placid atmosphere. The savory aroma was filling the room, making me crave the chef's dinner platter right from tea time. The slow murmurs in the room soon replaced them with pandemonium, with data being transferred from one head to another, which seemed too chaotic after a long, muted pandemic. The conversations were other than global warming and stock speculation.

After spending 2 minutes of quiet coffee time to myself, as the commercial cacophony jarred into my ears, I pushed myself into the mingling crowd, everybody trumping their own horns.

Me: I'm... I can remove your facial dark spots.

She: Oh! I'm... I can promote you a lot by creating strong ad spots.

Then I came across a gym owner. As he began explaining to me the importance of practicing resistance training with the tongue in the cheek,

I replied: My mind always practices resistance towards training, meetings, and networking. Does it count?"

As my socializing battery got drained, I plugged myself into an Uber cab, driving myself straight to my silent home. Quickly, a forgetful me, I sat down for an hour to pen down the minutes of the meeting while playing, 'I did it my way' in the background, creating a placid atmosphere. I concluded the minutes with: 'Everybody's business brief seemed original and good. Only the original parts were not good, and good parts didn't seem original.' Wondering how to remove dark spots from the ad spots, I called off the day and made my way to the bed.

Today, when another business conclave is lined up, I'm reiterating my last conclave talk: 'Let's do something together soon', and suddenly six months have passed without a single phone call. Others have found their business partners and soulmates, and I'm still auditioning! I realized I'm enthusiastically running my exquisite business; only my clients are bombastic and profits are playing gymnastics, and apart from work being a little classically chaotic, life is fantastic.

www.ingramcontent.com/pod-product-compliance
Lightning Source LLC
LaVergne TN
LVHW020449070526
838199LV00063B/4892